CELEBRITY CELIA

Level 5F

Written by Louise Goodman
Illustrated by Kimberley Scott

What is synthetic phonics?

Synthetic phonics teaches children to recognise the sounds of letters and to blend (synthesise) them together to make whole words.

Understanding sound/letter relationships gives children the confidence and ability to read unfamiliar words, without having to rely on memory or guesswork; this helps them to progress towards independent reading.

Did you know? Spoken English uses more than 40 speech sounds. Each sound is called a *phoneme*. Some phonemes relate to a single letter (d-o-g) and others to combinations of letters (sh-ar-p). When a phoneme is written down it is called a *grapheme*. Teaching these sounds, matching them to their written form and sounding out words for reading is the basis of synthetic phonics.

Consultant

I love reading phonics has been created in consultation with language expert Abigail Steel. She has a background in teaching and teacher training and is a respected expert in the field of synthetic phonics. Abigail Steel is a regular contributor to educational publications. Her international education consultancy supports parents and teachers in the promotion of literacy skills.

Reading tips

This book focuses on the s sound, made with the letter c when followed by e, i or y as in cent, circus and cyst.

Tricky words in this book

Any words in bold may have unusual spellings or are new and have not yet been introduced.

Tricky words in this book:

wants being who physicist please come

Extra ways to have fun with this book

After the reader has read the story, ask them questions about what they have just read:

What did Celia do on the stage?

Did you learn any new words in the book?

You're looking for the theatre? I'm sorry, I have no idea which way it is.

THEATRE

A pronunciation guide

This grid contains the sounds used in the stories in levels 4, 5 and 6 and a guide on how to say them. /a/ represents the sounds made, rather than the letters in a word.

/ai/ as in game	/ai/ as in play/they	/ee/ as in leaf/these	/ee/ as in he
/igh/ as in kite/light	/igh/ as in find/sky	/oa/ as in home	/oa/ as in snow
/oa/ as in cold	/y+oo/ as in cube/music/new	long /oo/ as in flute/crew/blue	/oi/ as in boy
/er/ as in bird/hurt	/or/ as in snore/oar/door	/or/ as in dawn/sauce/walk	/e/ as in head
/e/ as in said/any	/ou/ as in cow	/u/ as in touch	/air/ as in hare/bear/there
/eer/ as in deer/here/cashier	/t/ as in tripped/skipped	/d/ as in rained	/j/ as in gent/gin/gym
/j/ as in barge/hedge	/s/ as in cent/circus/cyst	/s/ as in prince	/s/ as in house
/ch/ as in itch/catch	/w/ as in white	/h/ as in who	/r/ as in write/rhino

Sounds this story focuses on
are highlighted in the grid.

/**f**/ as in phone	/**f**/ as in rough	/**ul**/ as in pencil/ hospital	/**z**/ as in fries/ cheese/breeze
/**n**/ as in knot/ gnome/engine	/**m**/ as in welcome /thumb/column	/**g**/ as in guitar/ghost	/**zh**/ as in vision/beige
/**k**/ as in chord	/**k**/ as in plaque/ bouquet	/**nk**/ as in uncle	/**ks**/ as in box/books/ ducks/cakes
/**a**/ and /**o**/ as in hat/what	/**e**/ and /**ee**/ as in bed/he	/**i**/ and /**igh**/ as in fin/find	/**o**/ and /**oa**/ as in hot/cold
/**u**/ and short /**oo**/ as in but/put	/**ee**/, /**e**/ and /**ai**/ as in eat/ bread/break	/**igh**/, /**ee**/ and /**e**/ as in tie/field/friend	/**ou**/ and /**oa**/ as in cow/blow
/**ou**/, /**oa**/ and /**oo**/ as in out/ shoulder/could	/**i**/ and /**ai**/ as in money/they	/**c**/ and /**s**/ as in cat/cent	/**y**/, /**igh**/ and /**i**/ as in yes/sky/myth
/**g**/ and /**j**/ as in got/giant	/**ch**/, /**c**/ and / **sh**/ as in chin/ school/chef	/**er**/, /**air**/ and /**eer**/ as in earth/bear/ears	/**u**/, /**ou**/ and /**oa**/ as in plough/dough

Be careful not to add an 'uh' sound to 's', 't', 'p',
'c', 'h', 'r', 'm', 'd', 'g', 'l', 'f' and 'b'. For example,
say 'fff' not 'fuh' and 'sss' not 'suh'.

Celia **wants** to be a celebrity
on the stage.

She imagines **being** a star —
riding a unicycle, playing the
cymbals, ice skating...

...but her parents, **who** are both professors, want her to be a **physicist**. So one day, Celia packs a bag and sets off to the theatre.

THEATRE

Celia begs the director to let her in the show. "Oh **please**, please," she cries.

"Hush!" says the director.
"I don't want any stress.
We'll give you a try."

Celia learns to ride a unicycle...

Clash the cymbals...
And skate on the ice!

Soon, Celia is the star
of the show!

Every night she performs more
and more amazing tricks...

She plays the cymbals on
the unicycle....

.She rides a unicycle on the ice...

She ice skates on a unicycle,
playing the cymbals — all at once!

Her talents never cease to amaze! But tonight, as Celia is about to go on stage...

she notices her parents!
"**Come** home, Celia," they say.

But Celia runs onto the stage.
She performs better than ever.

She skates, cycles and clashes her cymbals... she is fantastic!

"Hurray!" everyone shouts.

"Amazing!" say Celia's parents. "Let's celebrate! And you can stay on the stage, as long as you get home in time to do your homework."

Celia says yes. After all...

THE AMAZING PHYSICIST ★ CELIA! ★

...one day Celia might want to be a celebrity physicist!

OVER **48** TITLES IN SIX LEVELS
Abigail Steel recommends...

Some titles from Level 4

The Circus Mice — 978-1-84898-582-7

Monster's Night — 978-1-84898-583-4

The Mummy Code — 978-1-84898-585-8

Other titles to enjoy from Level 5

The Gigantic Bear — 978-1-84898-586-5

The Cemetery Dance — 978-1-84898-588-9

Goose Flight — 978-1-84898-589-6

Some titles from Level 6

Hugh is New — 978-1-84898-590-2

Clumsy Eagle — 978-1-84898-591-9

Bad Zombie Movie — 978-1-84898-592-6

An Hachette UK Company
www.hachette.co.uk

Copyright © Octopus Publishing Group Ltd 2012
First published in Great Britain in 2012 by TickTock, an imprint of Octopus Publishing Group Ltd,
Endeavour House, 189 Shaftesbury Avenue, London WC2H 8JY.
www.octopusbooks.co.uk

ISBN 978 1 84898 587 2

Printed and bound in China
10 9 8 7 6 5 4 3 2 1